Little Witch

Little Witch

BY

ANNA ELIZABETH BENNETT

ILLUSTRATED BY

HELEN STONE

A TRUMPET CLUB SPECIAL EDITION

Published by The Trumpet Club
666 Fifth Avenue, New York, New York 10103

ISBN: 0-440-84278-6

This edition published by arrangement
with Harper & Row, Publishers, Inc.
Printed in the United States of America
October 1990

10 9 8 7 6 5 4 3 2 1
OPM

CONTENTS

1

THE BLACK SPELL BREW

The ugliest, most rickety house in town belonged to the old witch, Madam Snickasnee. It stood on the very edge of the town, a small, melancholy house with steps so old that one was in danger of falling through them; but Madam Snickasnee was too busy working her black magic and riding around on her broomstick to do anything about it—even if she had wanted to.

She had a daughter, however, who hated the house, and looked with longing at the gay, neat houses of the town. Her name was Minikin—Minx for short; she was nine years old, and she wished with all her heart that she were not a witch's child.

Little Witch

This evening Madam Snickasnee was preparing as usual for her nightly jaunt on her broomstick to see what trouble she could stir up.

"Don't you want to come along with me, tonight?" she asked, in her harsh crow-voice. "You haven't been out riding in a week!"

"No, I don't," said Minx. "I don't like riding around in the dark and cold."

"You disobedient girl!" shrieked the old witch. "You're no child of mine! You'll have to start changing your ways pretty soon or you won't grow up into a decent witch!" She glared at Minx with her little red eyes, clapping her tall, pointed hat on her scraggly hair.

"Well, as long as you're feeling so high-and-mighty," she went on, "you can just get to work and cook up a pot of Black Spell Brew, and if you don't do it, you won't get anything to eat tomorrow!"

Minx watched with relief as the witch sailed out the open door, up into the dark sky.

After a while, the girl went over to a cracked mirror, and leaning her arms on the ancient bureau beneath it, gazed at her reflection intently. She saw a thin, delicate face, a wide, soft mouth, and big eyes as dark as ripe blueberries. She had a dimple stuck in her chin, which she did not like, wishing it had been placed in her cheek, instead. But even magic could not change that now. Rummaging through a drawer of the bureau, she found

a somewhat toothless comb and ran it through her black hair, smoothing it around her shoulders. Then suddenly she gave a little jump and gasp, turning around swiftly.

"Oh! I know I saw her! I know I did!" she said aloud to the empty room. "That's happened so many times when I'm looking in the mirror." She stared eagerly into the mirror again. "I'll be looking in the mirror like this, and then all of a sudden, I think I see a lady in there— the most beautiful lady in the world, looking over my shoulder. But I'm never quick enough to see her for sure."

She sighed. "Well, I've got to go cook up the Black Spell Brew."

She took down the magic pot from a shelf, and placed it on the stove. It was an old-fashioned stove that had to be fed with wood in order to cook anything. She got the blaze started, and then went to fetch the jar of magic powder to make the brew.

"Oh dear! I wish I didn't have to do this!" she said. "The witch must be going to enchant some more children. As if we didn't have enough right here in this house!"

She went over to the wide window sill on which stood seven flowerpots. In each pot grew a different kind of flower. These, however, were not ordinary flowers; they were children of the town who had been enchanted into flowers-in-pots because they had been rude to Madam Snickasnee. Minx took great care to keep them watered and in good condition. She wished she could discover the magic formula to change them back into children.

"You poor things," she said to the flowers, "I hope you don't feel unhappy. I wish I could help you. I wish you were all children again, and then maybe you would play with me!"

The flowers seemed to stir a little bit, and Minx was sure they understood. She was so lonely for children to play with, because all the children in the town were afraid of the witch's child.

Suddenly her face brightened. "I'm not going to make that horrible old brew yet! I'm going to work on my experiment!"

She looked over all the jars of magic powders and liquids on the shelves. There were hundreds of them, all different colors. Almost every night when Madam Snickasnee went out, Minx worked on her experiment trying out a different powder each time. She was trying to make the right kind of magic to cause a fairy to appear. She had never seen a fairy, and she was very eager to have such a delightful experience. So far nothing had happened except once when a lot of toads started hopping out of the kettle, and another time when some large balloons floated into the room. Every time she tried her experiment she felt rather nervous because she did not know what might come of it.

The witch's big black cat, Scorcher, came into the room and rubbed against her legs. He had very wicked yellow eyes, and Minx felt as if he knew what she was up to.

"Go away, Scorcher, that's a good cat," she said, although she added privately to herself that he certainly was not a good cat. He scratched and bit and made himself a pig over song birds.

In a little while she had her magic liquid bubbling merrily in the pot. It was a delightful pink color, and Minx was almost sure that it was the right mixture this time.

The room became filled with vapor, and pretty soon a shape began to form above the stove. Minx could feel her heart hammering against her chest, and she squeezed her hands together anxiously. What would it be this time? Oh, would it— Oh, could it be a fairy?

First appeared a funny pointed face with big ears and slanting eyes; then a child's body down to the waist, and then—for goodness sake! The rest was the shape of a colt! Half boy and half horse he was, and he leaped

The Black Spell Brew

swiftly out of the kettle, landing with a clatter on the floor.

"What—what are you?" asked Minx, uneasily.

"I'm a centaur, of course, stupid," he said. "Half boy, half horse, that's me!"

Scorcher's back was arched, his fur stood on end, and he was spitting ferociously.

"Be quiet, you fiend," said the little centaur.

Scorcher leaped at him, claws outstretched; but the centaur thumped him firmly on the head with a solid hoof, so that Scorcher lay stunned for a few minutes.

"I can't stand cats with such sour dispositions," said the centaur. "Now please tell me, miss, why you chose to conjure me up?"

" 'Conjure'?" repeated Minx, blankly.

"That means 'to call forth by magic,' stupid," said the centaur. "And you'd better make your request pretty snappy because soon I'll be fading off back to Mythicalia."

"Oh, I—I don't have any request," stammered Minx. "I was just trying out an experiment."

"Oh, you were!" said the centaur, sneeringly. "And I had to make this trip for nothing!"

"I was just trying to make a fairy appear," explained Minx, humbly.

"A fairy!" hooted the centaur, throwing back his head and laughing wildly. "Why in the name of Pan would anyone ever waste their time on those silly little pests!

The Black Spell Brew

Pains in the neck they are, and when you think of all the disgusting stuff which has been written about them! Tons of it! Oh, my oats and hay! You're wasting your time, sweetheart!"

Minx glared at him, indignantly. "Well, I don't care what you think. You're just jealous, you nasty old centaur!"

The centaur leaped at her, and she drew back in fright. "Have a care!" he said, lifting a threatening hoof. "Remember what happened to your old cat! And see that you don't go conjuring me up again! I was just in the midst of a delicious dinner!"

His voice became fainter, and he began to grow misty around the edges. With a thankful heart, Minx watched him disappear altogether. Quickly she washed out the magic pot and put it back on the shelf. She knew that if she did not make the Black Spell Brew her mother would be horribly angry; but she was very tired, and wanted to go to bed.

She went over to a ragged blanket that was spread out on the floor, and lay down.

"I wish— Oh, I wish I could see a fairy," she thought, drowsily. "I wish I had some children to play with . . .

Little Witch

I wish I knew who the lady in the mirror is . . . I wish I could change the flowerpot children back . . . I wish I wasn't a witch's child."

And then she took her wishes with her into sleep.

2

BRAVE MINIKIN

Madam Snickasnee was most certainly outraged the next morning when she discovered that Minx had not prepared the brew.

"Lazy good-for-nothing!" she stormed. "Pray tell what *did* you do with your time last night?"

"I slept," said Minx.

"Slept! Well, if you're going to be a proper witch you'll have to learn to do your sleeping in the daytime like other respectable witches. You're just not cut out to be a witch, I guess! But I'll see to it that you mend your ways or I'll change you into a flowerpot, or maybe something much less pretty!"

Little Witch

Minx shuddered and glanced over at the seven flower-pots on the window sill.

"I said you wouldn't get anything to eat today, and I'll keep my word!" continued Madam Snickasnee. "I'm going to make a delicious breakfast of toads on toast before I go to bed, and after that I'm going to lock all the food up. Then maybe you'll do as I tell you the next time!"

Minx knew better than to argue; so she said nothing. She felt very hungry as she watched the witch gobble down her breakfast. She was not fond of toads, but she would have eaten anything this morning, as her stomach felt so empty.

She heard the schoolbell ringing, and thought, as she did every day, how much she would love to go to school. She had never been to school, and she had no idea what they did there; but it would be fun to be with other children. If only they would not run away from her!

Presently she heard her mother's snores rattling from the blanket on the floor, and she went swiftly to the door. Today she was going to do something important—something brave.

Quickly she slipped outside, shutting the door quietly

behind her. Her heart beating furiously, she walked rapidly up the road toward the schoolhouse. Oh, if only, if only they would not run away from her this time! She saw some wild asters growing by the road, and stopped to pick some. Swiftly she twined them in her dark hair. They made her look odder than ever; but she didn't know this; she thought only that she must look less like a witch's child.

When she arrived at the red brick schoolhouse, she looked at it fearfully.

"Maybe I'd better not go today," she said to herself. "Maybe I'd better come back tomorrow."

Then it seemed as if she almost heard a voice whisper: "Go in, go in NOW."

She looked around, but could see no one. Then she walked slowly into the building, pausing inside the door, quite bewildered. It was such a wide hall, and there were so many doors. Where should she go? Just then she saw a man coming toward her.

"Where you belong, sister?" he asked, in a friendly tone of voice.

"I—I don't know," said Minx. "Are you the head one?"

Little Witch

The man laughed, smothering the sound behind a large red hand. "Say, sister," he said, "I guess you're new here. I'm Mr. Noddle, the janitor. I guess you need to go see the principal. Come along with me."

Looking around timidly, Minx followed the kindly Mr. Noddle along the hall. Some of the doors were open, and she could see children sitting in classrooms. At last Mr. Noddle led her into the principal's office, and explained to the young lady at the desk that it was a new girl.

The young lady took her in to the principal.

"Mr. Bunch, this is a new girl," explained the young lady, and left her there.

Mr. Bunch was sitting behind a large, cluttered desk, staring at her fiercely from beneath thick, black eyebrows. He had a mustache which was even thicker, and if possible, blacker, and every now and then he would lasso one end of the mustache with his tongue, and chew on it hungrily.

Minx gazed at him in fascinated terror.

Finally Mr. Bunch spoke. His voice was as bristly as his mustache.

"Well, young lady, what is your name?"

"Minx." Her voice sounded weak and wobbly.

"Minx what?"

"Well, it's really Minikin. Minikin Snickasnee."

Mr. Bunch's eyes popped. "The witch's child!" he roared.

Minx started to back toward the door. But again she seemed to hear the voice whisper, "Don't be a sissy. Stand up to him!"

She shut her mouth into a firm line, raised her head, and fixed Mr. Bunch with a long, defiant look. Then she said, "I want to go to school. I have a right to, haven't I?"

Little Witch

Mr. Bunch passed a trembling hand across his forehead. "Why—why of course you have. In fact," he glared at Minx again, "why haven't you been to school before?"

"My mother wouldn't let me come," said Minx. "But today I just made up my mind I would."

"Your mother will find herself in a fine pot of trouble," grumbled Mr. Bunch, "if she breaks the law!"

Minx tried to picture Madam Snickasnee in a pot of trouble; but instead she saw other people stewing in Madam's pot—Mr. Bunch, for one.

"Can you read?" asked Mr. Bunch.

"No."

"Then you'll have to go into the first grade," said Mr. Bunch, "and learn with the babies."

This did not bother Minx very much, until the young lady took her to the first grade, and she saw the little children staring at her in surprise. She felt very silly, such a big girl, among these little ones. But she thought, "I don't care. I'm going to learn, too."

The teacher, Miss Taylor, was young and kind, although she seemed rather scared of Minx.

At recess time Minx ran outdoors with the others.

Little Witch

She looked around to find children of her own age. At last she saw some girls playing jacks, and she started toward them; but as soon as they saw her, they ran away, screaming, "Oh, the witch child! Run! Run! The witch child!"

Minx fought to keep back the tears. But she was feeling very weak from hunger, and at last she could be brave no longer. She leaned her head against the wall of the school building, and sobbed.

Suddenly she heard a shy, sweet voice say, "Why are you crying?" and looking up, she saw a girl about her own age. This girl had a round, cheerful face with pink cheeks, and wide gray eyes. Her smooth yellow hair was tied back with a perky pink bow.

Minx wiped away her tears and said, "I'm Minx, the witch's child. Aren't you afraid of me?"

"No, I'm not," said the girl, calmly. "I've often wanted to talk to you because I think it must be very interesting to be a witch's child. Isn't it?"

"No, it's not," said Minx, gloomily. "I wish I wasn't a witch's child."

"Here," said the girl, producing some cookies from her pocket. "Would you like these?"

Minx snatched them hungrily and started stuffing them in her mouth.

The girl stared. "My goodness, you act as if you haven't eaten all day!" she said.

"I haven't," said Minx. "My mother is punishing me."

Just then the bell rang for the end of recess.

"Meet me after school," said the girl. "My name is Frances. Maybe you'd like to come home with me."

"Oh yes!" cried Minx, joyfully.

The afternoon seemed endless to Minx, and at dismissal time, she started to rush out to meet Frances, but Miss Taylor detained her.

"Minx," she said, nervously, "when you come tomorrow, be sure to wash yourself well, and wear a clean dress."

Minx looked at her in great surprise. "But I only have this one dress," she said.

Miss Taylor seemed distressed. "Well, please, Minx," she said, "wash it out over the week end."

"Yes, all right," promised Minx, anxious to meet Frances.

At last the two girls were walking toward Frances's home, and Frances was asking all sorts of questions.

Little Witch

When Minx told her about the magic kettle, Frances's face sparkled.

"Oh, how exciting it would be to have a magic kettle! Couldn't you let me see it some day?"

To think that this wonderful girl wanted to come to her house! Minx felt as if there were wings wafting her along.

At last they came to Frances's house, and it was just the sort of house that Minx wished she lived in: white and green, spruce and gay, with a garden all around.

"Just wait till you meet my great-grandmother!" said Frances. "You'll wish you never had to go home again!"

Minx was wishing that already, with all her heart.

3

THE FLYING BROOMSTICK

Frances led the way into the kitchen, stepping expertly over a scooter, a pair of skates, and a pile of building blocks.

"Grandma," she said, "here's my new friend, Minx."

Grandma looked up from the small boy over whom she was bending, vigorously scrubbing his neck.

Minx was a bit startled to see that she had a hat on—a remarkable hat with gay piles of fruit and intertwining leaves. But it could not quite hide her silver-white hair, and it seemed to accentuate the blue of her eyes and the pink of her cheeks.

Her smile shone from her face like a star, as she said, gaily, "Hello, Minx! I'm glad to see you. Stop squirming, George! I don't believe you've washed your neck in a week!"

The Flying Broomstick

George was struggling to escape the washcloth, and at the same time trying to observe the visitor.

He was blond and round-faced like his sister, and about six years old.

"Why have you got your hat on, Grandma?" asked Frances.

"I was just on my way down to the library. But when I saw George's neck I knew I couldn't set foot outside this house till I washed it!"

She released the resentful George.

"It's not that I mind necks a little bit dirty, but when they get *that* black—"

She was interrupted by a terrible commotion just outside, and then three more children, all fair haired and rosy, came piling in, everyone talking at the same time.

"Here are my sister Alice and my brothers Bob and Jack," said Frances. "Alice is five, Bob is seven, and Jack is eight. Kids, this is my new friend, Minx."

"How lovely to have such a large family," said Minx, enviously.

"Yes, lovely!" said Grandma. "But I don't get a moment to breathe, hardly. Their mother and father are dead, and I take care of them, singlehanded. I really love doing it, but I wish I had some time to give to my painting."

"Grandma loves to paint," explained Frances. "She just took it up last year, but she doesn't have much time to do it."

"Wait till we grow up, Gram," piped George.

Grandma laughed. "Yes! I'll be only about ninety then! Well, I've got to be going. Have fun, children, and don't wreck the house *too* much!"

After she had left, Bob, who had been staring intently at Minx, said, "Say—I know who you are. You're the witch child!"

Alice gave a shriek.

"Oh Alice, don't be silly," said Frances. "Minx is a very nice girl. She won't hurt you."

Both Alice and George backed away, fearfully.

"Say," said Jack, "tell us what it's like to be a witch."

"I don't like to be a witch," said Minx, unhappily. "I'd like to be just like other children."

"But don't you know lots of magic?" persisted Jack.

"I know some," admitted Minx, rather proudly.

"Tell us," said Bob. "What sort of things can you do?"

"Well, I can put magic powders in my mother's kettle and strange things happen like balloons and toads and centaurs coming out."

"Gee!" said Bob.

"Can you ride on a broomstick?" asked George.

"Oh sure," said Minx, scornfully. "That's easy as pie!"

"Minx," said Frances, "do you suppose that some time you could let us ride on your broomstick?"

"Oh sure," said Minx. "I'll bring it to school tomorrow."

"And won't you let us see you stir up the magic in the kettle?" asked Bob.

Minx hesitated. "Well— you'd have to come at night."

"Oh, we could do that!" cried Jack.

"How could we, silly?" demanded Frances. "You know perfectly well that Grandma doesn't allow us out after dark!"

The faces of all the children fell, and groans proceeded from every bosom.

"I'm trying an experiment now," said Minx. "I'm trying to find just the right mixture to make a fairy appear."

Instantly everyone became excited again.

"Oh, we'll just *have* to go!" cried Frances. "Maybe Grandma will let us if we don't stay too late!"

Minx glanced out the window and noticed that it was getting dark. "I think I'd better go," she said, anxiously. "My mother will be waking up, and she'll be simply furious!"

"Oh, do you have to go yet?" cried Frances. "Just let me give you something to eat first!"

Minx was more than willing to wait for this, as she was feeling very groggy from hunger.

Frances quickly filled a large glass with milk and made her a thick sandwich with plenty of lettuce and peanut butter.

"Oh, gosh," said Minx, from a full mouth. "I never tasted anything so good!"

She ate two sandwiches, six cookies, and drank two glasses of milk. She had never eaten so much before at one meal, and her stomach felt very uncomfortable.

All the children accompanied her to the door and Jack even dragged the scooter out of her way.

"Are you going to work on your experiment tonight?" asked Frances.

"Just as soon as my mother leaves," said Minx. "She always goes when it gets dark."

"If we can, we'll come over. O.K.?" said Frances.

"O.K.!" said Minx. "I hope you can come!"

She ran swiftly through the darkening streets, hoping desperately that the witch would still be asleep.

But as soon as she hurried up the stairs, her heart sank to the soles of her feet for there was Madam Snickasnee standing in the doorway, her red eyes gleaming maliciously through the dark. Minx's first impulse was to turn and run like a hare; but Madam Snickasnee reached out a large, skinny hand and grabbed her by the ear.

"Come in here, you wicked thing!" she screeched. "Where have you been till this hour?"

Little Witch

Minx tried to speak, but the words seemed to shrivel in her throat.

"Well, where's your tongue, miss? Nothing to say, eh? Just remember the flowerpots! Don't take it for granted that you're so safe!"

With relief, Minx watched her pick up her broom and straddle it.

"I won't even ask you to come with me tonight," snarled Madam Snickasnee. "I wouldn't care for your high and mighty company. But see to it that tonight you make the Black Spell Brew, or something much worse will happen to you than just going hungry!"

With that threat, she soared off into the sky.

Minx sighed and went directly to the shelves to start preparing the Black Spell Brew. All sorts of dreadful things went into it, such as dried toads' and snakes' blood, and crushed toadstools.

As she stirred it and watched the horrible dark mixture bubble and steam, she felt very unhappy.

"I wish my mother would stop enchanting children," she thought. "Just think! Maybe she might even enchant Frances or her sister and brothers."

This thought struck her so hard that she forgot to

The Flying Broomstick

stir the brew, and stood horrified, staring into space.

Just then she heard a scuffling noise outside; next, a timid knock sounded on the door. Her heart leaped up in joy, for she knew it must be her new friends.

When she opened the door she saw that they were all there, from Frances down to Alice.

"Grandma said we could stay an hour," said Frances. "So let's hurry and try the experiment."

35

Little Witch

"I want to see a fairy," said Alice.

"Well, first I'll have to pour out this stuff and wash out the pot," said Minx.

She poured the Black Spell Brew into bottles while the children looked on curiously.

"What's that?" asked Jack.

"Oh that," said Minx, uncomfortably. "That's just a brew."

Bob wanted to know what kind of brew it was; but Minx pretended not to hear him.

"Now," she said, "we'll wash out the pot, and then we'll be all set to try the experiment! Maybe it will work tonight!"

4

THE WATER NIXIE

"Now," said Minx, "let me decide what powder to use this time!"

The children stood staring with round eyes at the rows and rows of mysterious bottles.

"Choose the green one!" cried George.

"No, take the blue!" begged Alice.

"George asked first, so I'll take green this time," said Minx.

She dumped some of the green into the magic kettle, and immediately it bubbled up into a frothy mass.

The children were silent with wonder as she stirred the green mixture.

"Don't you have to say any magic words while you do that?" asked Jack.

"Like 'abra-ca-dabra,' " said Bob.

"Oh my goodness," said Minx, loftily, "that's old-fashioned stuff. Witches don't do that sort of thing any more! In the old days they even used to have to go out and catch their own bats and toads and stuff to make their powders out of. Now it all comes out of bottles."

"Where do you buy them?" asked Frances.

"My mother sends for everything from the Witches' Market. That's located near the Never-Never Land. They send her a catalog, and she orders from that."

Now the vapor was filling the room, and something was taking shape.

The children were quiet as shadows, gazing in fascination. Alice, however, began to feel rather frightened, and started to move toward the door.

"Oh," said Minx, in a soft, breathless voice, "I believe it is— I believe it is!"

The face that appeared was thin and sharply pointed toward the chin. The skin was of the palest green, the eyes were large and filled with strange lights, and the hair was long, green, and dripping with water.

The Water Nixie

At last a slim girl body, draped in a clinging silvery green garment, took form, and leaped to the floor as lightly as a sunbeam.

"Are you a fairy?" asked Minx, tremulously.

"She has no wings," said George, skeptically.

The creature laughed with a sound like water splashing softly on pebbles.

"Of course I'm not a fairy, you funny child," she said. "Don't you know what I am?"

They all shook their heads, solemnly.

"I'm a nixie!" She danced around the room like a jet of spray.

"What's a nixie?" asked Alice.

"A nixie, poor ignorant girl child, is a sprite of the water."

"You mean—there are things—I mean people like you, living in the water?" said Frances.

"Of course! Only it's not often anyone is granted the wonderful privilege of seeing us. I hope you appreciate your good fortune!"

She began to leap and twirl again, light as spindrift.

"Oh, yes we do," said Frances, gravely.

The nixie finished her dance and said, "Now tell me what you want me for. I'm beginning to feel uncomfortably dry and warm, and I'll have to return to my lake soon."

"Well, I didn't really want you," said Minx.

The nixie looked quite hurt, and green tears began to slip down her cheeks. "You didn't really want to s-see me?"

The Water Nixie

"Oh, of course we're glad to see you," Minx reassured her, "but I've been trying and trying to make a fairy appear."

"Oh my goodness!" cried the nixie. "Fairies! They're so ordinary! I know simply hundreds of them, and they've got no more personality than a—than a clam shell!"

"But we would like to see one anyway," said Alice.

"Well—maybe I can help you! Why don't you try—"

At this moment, to the children's utter disappointment, the nixie became vapor again, and slipped through the window.

"Oh gosh!" said Jack. "Try getting her back, Minx!"

"She was just going to tell us!" said Frances.

"I'm afraid to use more of the powder," said Minx, "because my mother might notice it."

All the children looked downcast.

"But we can try again tomorrow night," said Minx, "if you can come."

"Oh, sure we can!" said Bob, promptly.

"That is—if we get home when we're supposed to, tonight," said Frances. "I think we'd better leave now."

"Maybe you'd better," said Minx, looking anxiously

at the bottle of Black Spell Brew, "because sometimes my mother comes home early."

At that, the children disappeared very suddenly through the door.

Minx sighed and put back the pot on the shelf. Then she went to the mirror, and gazed into it earnestly. "I haven't seen her today yet," she said, aloud. "Maybe I'll see her for sure tonight."

Suddenly she gave a little cry. There in the mirror —surely, oh surely it was a face! A beautiful face, pale as moonlight, with night-dark eyes, a flower-soft mouth. . . . Minx spun around quickly—but nothing was there!

She stood quite still in disappointment. Then she said, "Oh well, at least I'm sure I did see her tonight, and maybe tomorrow I'll see her outside the mirror!"

She felt very sleepy, and went over to her blanket. As she lay down, she thought, "Tomorrow I must remember to take my broomstick to school and let the children ride on it."

The next morning she awoke to find Madam Snick-asnee already seated at the cluttered table, chewing greedily on a fried bat's wing.

"So you're awake at last, are you, lazybones?" the witch greeted her. "I see you finally obeyed me and made the brew!"

Minx seized a piece of bread and began to chew it hungrily.

"Have some manners!" screamed the witch. "Eat like a lady!"

Although there was no clock in the house, Minx thought it must be time to get ready for school. She recalled what her teacher had told her, and going to the sink, started to splash water on her face and arms, half-heartedly.

Madam Snickasnee was so astonished that she stopped chewing for a few seconds.

"What are you doing that for?" she demanded.

"Oh, I just felt like it." Minx tried to sound casual.

"You're up to something, my lass. Don't tell me you're not. You just stay right in this house today, and don't you dare stir out of it!"

"Yes, Ma'am," said Minx, as innocent as an angel right out of heaven.

"You look too innocent, my girl! Just remember what I said!"

Little Witch

Madam Snickasnee tossed a well-polished bone to Scorcher, who pounced on it and started to crunch it noisily.

Minx heard the schoolbell ring, and her heart sank in despair.

"Oh, why doesn't she hurry up and go to sleep!" she thought. But she knew that if her mother discovered how anxious she felt that she would stay awake on purpose all day.

Humming a tuneless tune, Minx went to water the unhappy flowerpots.

"That reminds me," said Madam Snickasnee, darkly, fixing her little red eyes on the bottle of Black Spell Brew.

Minx's hand trembled a bit, but she continued to hum.

"Oh, please, please go to sleep," she thought, desperately.

But presently the witch's eyelids began to droop, and her head to sink down on her bony chest. At last with a thud her head dropped to the table, and the dishes began to clatter and clink with the violence of her snores.

Thankfully, Minx grabbed her broom and rushed out of the house.

Little Witch

"I'm late, I'm late," she thought, fearfully. "I wonder what they'll do to me!"

She was running with furious speed along the road, when suddenly she stopped short.

"My goodness!" she said. "Here I am wasting my breath on running when I could be riding!"

So she flung one slim leg over her broomstick, gave a little push with her foot, and up, up she went, into the clear October sky, riding swiftly toward the schoolhouse.

Mr. Bunch, looking out of his office window, was certainly surprised to see his newest pupil arriving in such an unusual fashion.

5

MR. BEANPOT, DETECTIVE

When Minx walked into the classroom, Miss Taylor said, "Minx, you're late. And whatever have you brought a broom with you for?"

"I'm going to let the children take rides on it during recess," said Minx.

Miss Taylor looked disconcerted. "Why—I'm sure that's very nice of you, Minx, but—but I really don't think Mr. Bunch would allow it."

Groans of disappointment rolled through the room.

Miss Taylor clapped her hands. "Now children, stop that noise! Go to your seat, Minx, and be on time tomorrow. Let's get on with our reading!"

Little Witch

Minx placed her broom in the wardrobe, and obediently took her seat. While she was learning how to read such words as "cat," "dog," and "boy," she forgot all about the broom.

The other boys and girls, however, did not forget it. As soon as they were released for recess, they crowded around Minx, excitedly.

"Oh Minx, please let me ride on the broom!"

"Please Minx, let me!"

Minx looked around to see if Mr. Bunch or Miss Taylor was in sight, and as all was clear, she handed the broom to one of the small boys.

"Here. Just sit on it and give a push and it'll go up. Then when you want to come down, just say 'down please.' It will go wherever you tell it to."

The small boy flung a chubby leg over, and up he went, looking scared. He came down very soon, rather pale and shaken, and handed the broom meekly to the next child. Up she spun, laughing and shrieking, and she stayed so long whizzing about above the trees, that they all began to shout for her to come down.

The fun and excitement were becoming uproarious when suddenly Mr. Bunch appeared in their midst. All

morning he had been unable to do a jot of work, so pre-occupied was he with the thought of Minikin Snickasnee coming to school on a broomstick. Should he speak to her or shouldn't he? As a matter of fact, he felt quite odd about the child; nervous, in truth. But just now when he had seen, out of his window, these goings on, he had made up his mind.

Now he roared, "STOP THIS NONSENSE!"

Instantly everyone was silenced. Up in the air a girl was still riding around, gaily.

"COME DOWN HERE!" shouted Mr. Bunch. Immediately the girl came hurtling down, bumping against the ground rather hard.

"What nonsense is this?" boomed Mr. Bunch. "Minikin Snickasnee, you are the cause of all this!"

Minx had an urge to run; but looking around for an opening in the crowd, she saw Frances smiling at her.

Then bravely she turned and faced Mr. Bunch.

"I didn't mean to make any trouble," she said, unhappily. "I promise I won't ever do it again."

"See to it that you leave that—that infernal broom at home, hereafter," commanded Mr. Bunch, "because if I ever see it again, I'll take it away from you!"

Minx nodded, miserably. Just when she was getting to be friends with all these children! Now they would probably make fun of her all the more.

Mr. Bunch marched off, indignantly, and the children drifted away, in silence. At that moment the bell rang for the end of recess.

"I'll wait for you after school!" called Frances.

When Minx joined her friend after school, Frances said, "Never mind about the broomstick. Some of the kids got rides, anyway."

"Oh, I can give you rides on Saturday," said Minx, "if you don't think it would make you into a witch!"

Frances laughed merrily. "Silly! You have to be born a witch to be one!"

"Oh, if only I hadn't been born a witch!" mourned Minx. "I sometimes dream that my mother isn't really a witch, but a beautiful fairy."

"You don't look like a witch," said Frances, comfortingly. "Maybe your mother will reform. Grandma once read us a book about a pirate who did. Maybe witches can too, sometimes!"

"Well, I certainly hope so," said Minx, doubtfully.

"Can you come home with me today?" asked Frances.

"Not today. I'd better not," said Minx. "My mother was very angry last night because I was out."

"What did she do to you?"

"Just hollered around. But she might get mad enough to change me into something."

Frances's eyes widened. "Oh Minx! How awful! Would she change all of us into something if she found us there?"

Minx looked very unhappy. "Well—yes, she would," she admitted. "She'd change you into flowerpots!"

"Maybe we'd better not come anymore," said Frances, in a scared voice.

"Maybe you'd better not," agreed Minx, her heart heavy with disappointment.

When she left Frances, she felt so dejected that she walked along slowly, dragging her broom in the dust.

She was so wrapped up in her gloomy thoughts that she did not see the man who suddenly stepped out in front of her, until she bumped into him.

"Oops, sis," said he, and she looked up to see a short, stout man in a bright plaid suit, with a large cigar stuck in one corner of his mouth.

Never having been taught manners, she did not even

think of apologizing, and as he did not step out of her way, she stood staring at him, curiously.

"Pardon me, sis," said the man, breezily. "Ain't you the daughter of Madam Snickasnee?"

Immediately Minx felt apprehensive. "Yes, I am."

"Well, I'm Mr. Beanpot, Master Detective," he said, importantly.

Minx eyed him, fearfully.

"There's a little matter of some missing children from the town," said Mr. Beanpot, staring down at Minx, with small, accusing gray eyes. "You wouldn't know about them, would you?"

"M-missing children?" stammered Minx, flushing.

"Seven to be exact," said Mr. Beanpot, holding up seven fat, pink fingers, "and their parents are missing 'em horribly." He added thoughtfully, "Though for the life o' me, I can't see why Billy Martin's family'd ever miss him except pleasantly." He shook his head, disapprovingly.

Minx edged around him, carefully, getting set to run; but Mr. Beanpot was too alert for her. He reached out a pudgy hand and grasped her arm.

"Hold on there, sis. Aside from the question of Billy

Martin—your mother is under suspicion. You wouldn't know about those kids, would you?"

"N-no, I wouldn't." Her knees were shaking.

"Well, I'll be around, sis. And if I find out your mother is the kidnaper, it's jail for her—and for you, too!"

He poked his round red nose threateningly in her frightened face. "And you tell your mother what I said!"

Suddenly, her courage returned, and straightening her back, she said, defiantly, "Why don't you tell her yourself?"

It was Mr. Beanpot's turn to look nervous. "Why—er—uh." He mopped his face with a large purple handkerchief. "Never you mind gettin' fresh, sis! Jest remember what I told you!"

As Minx proceeded on her way, she muttered, "Fraidy-cat! 'fraid of a witch!"

When she arrived home, she was relieved to see that the witch had not yet awakened. Her snores were rattling the window shades.

Minx hid her schoolbooks in the bottom of a bureau drawer, and stared hopefully into the ancient mirror. But this time she could see nothing but her own thin, sad face.

Mr. Beanpot, Detective

When Madam Snickasnee woke up she was in a more frightful mood than usual, stamping around, screaming and throwing things here and there, but mostly at Minx. Minx was so clever at dodging that she was not struck once; but she was greatly relieved to see the witch float away at last into the darkening sky.

Minx made haste to start preparations for her nightly experiment. She felt very sorrowful that her friends would not be with her this evening.

"But maybe it's just as well," she thought.

At that moment, her heart gave a leap. There was a knock on the door! She rushed to answer it, and there stood all five children!

"Oh, I thought you weren't coming!" she cried, joyfully.

"We thought we wouldn't be sissies," said Frances. "We just couldn't stay away. Grandma sent you some cookies."

Without delay, Minx began devouring the cookies. She had never tasted anything so good in all her life.

"Hurry up! Hurry up!" cried Bob. "Let's get started!"

"What color would you like?" asked Minx, her mouth quite full.

Little Witch

"It's my turn! It's my turn!" cried Alice.

"O.K., Alice, you choose," said Minx.

"Let's see . . ." Alice stood so long deciding that the others became impatient. "Hurry up, Alice! Oh, hurry up, slow-poke!"

At last Alice cried, triumphantly, "I choose the yellow-and-red!"

6

ENCHANTED FLOWERPOTS

It was queer that although Minx stirred the mixture quite vigorously, the yellow and red never mingled. The red stayed on one side of the kettle, the yellow on the other.

"I can't understand it," said Jack, greatly perplexed. "It ought to be a funny brownish color right now. That's the way my paints do, anyhow."

"Sh!" said Frances, because now the mysterious vapor was beginning to rise from the pot, and slowly fill the whole room.

In fascination, the children watched the vapor shape itself into a strange sort of man wearing a long coat that was yellow on one side and red on the other. He was tall and thin with blond hair falling to his shoulders, and small, sharp blue eyes. He was holding a flute to his lips and blowing a soft, sweet sound through it.

He stepped with dignity to the floor, smiling merrily.

"Ah! Children! My weakness!" he said, in a rich, jolly voice. "Shall I play you a tune on my flute?"

"Wait a minute, please!" said Frances. "Aren't you the Pied Piper of Hamelin?"

"The same," he said, bowing very low.

"No tune for us then, thank you," said Frances, shaking her head at him, reprovingly. "We don't care to be spirited away by your flute playing as those other children were."

The Pied Piper looked at her in wounded astonishment. "Why, my dear young lady! I wouldn't dream of such a thing!"

"What happened to those other kids?" asked Jack.

"My dear boy," said the Pied Piper, "they are in a most delightful place. Most delightful! They have never grown any older than they were on that day so long ago, and they have everything their hearts desire: toys, good things to eat—everything!"

"But their poor mothers and fathers, how sad you made them!" said Frances.

"Ah, my sweet young lady, don't fret your pretty head about that ! Everything is lovely again. From the goodness of my heart, I forgave the townspeople who played such a low trick on me, and the mothers and fathers are again with their children."

"And the little lame boy who was too slow to get inside the hill?" persisted Frances.

"He is there, too, although grown up, of course," said the Pied Piper. "But he is lame no longer."

"Well, that's a relief!" Frances sighed, contentedly.

"Now that all those weighty matters are cleared up," said the Pied Piper, "pray tell me, young ladies and gentlemen, what do you wish of me?"

"Nothing, I guess," said Minx. "I was really trying to make a fairy appear!"

"Oh ho! Well, you must have done the wrong sort of things—whatever it is you do to make thingamajigs appear. But isn't there anything at all I could do for you?"

Minx shook her head. "No, I can't think of a thing!"

"While you're thinking some more, I'll take a stroll

around the kitchen," said the Pied Piper. "M-m-m, do I see cookies here?" He picked up one and sampled it with great concentration. "Oh boy! as they say nowadays. Someone around here is a good cook!"

"Grandma," said Bob, with pride.

"Lucky children to have such a grandma!" said the Pied Piper, solemnly.

Then his eyes lighted on the window sill.

"My, my! What an array of flowerpots!" he said. "Lovely—but there's something rather odd about them!"

Minx squirmed inside, recalling Mr. Beanpot.

"Yes," continued the Pied Piper. "These flowers look almost human!"

Suddenly Minx's face sparkled. "Say! Mr. Pied Piper, you're good at putting magic spells on children. Do you s'pose you could do something about changing these flowerpots back into children?"

"Oh ho!" cried the Pied Piper, his face lighting in understanding. "So that's why these plants look so human! What is this, the house of a witch?"

"Y-yes, my mother is," admitted Minx, nervously. "But please, Mr. Pied Piper, could you change them back into children?"

Enchanted Flowerpots

The Pied Piper's eyes twinkled as he looked at her.

"I'll try," he said, raising his flute to his lips. But just then he began to grow blurry around the edges, and fade slowly away.

"Oh, golly!" cried Jack. "Can't you do something, Minx?"

For a second Minx just stood there, wringing her hands in despair. Then she rushed to the shelf, and grabbed the jar of red and yellow powder.

"Just a speck more ought to bring 'im back!" she said, and tossed some more into the magic pot.

Breathlessly the children watched as the Pied Piper wavered, then slowly became more distinct, and once more there he was again, solid as he should be.

"Saved in the nick!" he said. "And now I'll see what I can do!"

Placing the flute to his lips, he blew a thin, sweet note.

As if their heads were pulled by strings simultaneously, the children looked at the flowerpots. Nothing was happening.

The Pied Piper next started to blow a merry, rollicking tune that made the children's feet go tap-tap-tap.

And then the strange thing happened! All the flower-pots began to change shape. They became misty around the sides, then they seemed to swell up and out, and in a very short time they were no longer flowerpots, but seven children on the window sill, squeezed much too closely together for comfort. They all looked quite dazed, and several of them were rubbing their eyes.

Finally the oldest boy spoke. "What's going on? What am I doing here?"

"Don't you remember?" asked Minx, in surprise.

"I can't remember a thing," said a girl. "Goodness, it's crowded on this window sill! What are we sitting here for?"

The children got down, still looking very bewildered.

"I feel so stiff in my legs," said a small boy, "as if I was sitting on them."

"Don't you remember?" said Frances. "You were—"

"SHHH!" whispered Minx, quickly. "Don't tell them, Frances!"

Frances looked at her with astonishment; but Minx frowned and shook her head.

"Well, young ladies and gentlemen," said the Pied Piper, "I have performed my little task, and I can feel myself becoming rather vaporous again. I trust you are satisfied?"

"Oh, thank you, Mr. Pied Piper," said Minx. "Now I guess the detective won't be able to put me in jail, after all!"

The Pied Piper's eyebrows shot up, questioningly; but before Minx could explain, he had faded quite away, every red and yellow speck of him, every flute note.

The seven children were looking around very curiously.

"Where are we, anyway?" demanded a boy, who happened to be the notorious Billy Martin.

"Never mind where you are," said Minx, pertly. "You'd better go home right away!"

"Well, you don't have to tell us where we are," said Billy, giving her a bold stare, "because I know who you are, anyway. You're the witch's daughter!"

The other children shrank back in alarm. The smallest boy began to cry.

"Oh, you needn't be so scared!" said Minx, in annoyance. "If it wasn't for me, you'd still be—" She remembered in time, and clapped a hand over her mouth.

"We'd still be what?" demanded Billy Martin, suspiciously.

"Never mind what," said Frances. "Why don't you just go home and keep quiet?"

"Keep quiet yourself!" said Billy. "Say you know what I think?"

"I'm not interested," Minx informed him.

But Billy persisted. "I think you put some kind of

a spell on us kids, that's what I think! You're a witch, too!"

"She is not!" Frances defended her friend, hotly.

"She is too!" said Billy. "And I think there's something funny going on around here!"

"Why don't you go home!" said Minx.

"I'm going, don't worry, but you ain't seen the last of me!"

Billy and the other ex-flowerpots went out, looking rather dazed.

"Now what do you suppose will happen?" said Minx, unhappily.

"Don't worry," Frances comforted her. "We'll stick by you, won't we, kids?"

Every head nodded vigorously. "We sure will, Minx!"

But Minx still looked anxious. "Even if they never remember they were flowerpots," she said, "they'll make everyone think they were under a spell. That Billy Martin surely will. Oh, why was I ever born a witch's child!"

7

THE BIRTHDAY CAKE

The next day was Saturday, and as soon as Madam Snickasnee was busily employed in manufacturing snores, Minx stripped off her clothes, and draped a long, old cape around her shoulders to protect herself from the chill air. Then she dumped her dirty clothes in the sink, and washed them as well as she could, without soap. Madam Snickasnee could not see the value of soap, as she never felt it necessary either to take a bath or wash her clothes. As for dishes, they were occasionally lightly rinsed off underneath the faucet.

Minx rubbed and scrubbed, now and then heaving a sigh of deep despair. Would they ever get clean?

The Birthday Cake

Finally, she decided that they never would, but at least they were about ten shades lighter. Then she wrung them out and took them outdoors, draping them over a low branch on the lone tree which stood in their tiny front yard.

"There now," she thought, with satisfaction.

It was such a bright, keen October day that she felt full of energy and big plans.

"I guess first I'd better go water the plants, poor thi—OH!" She stopped dead still in the front yard, one hand over her mouth, her eyes round with horror.

"Golly! I never thought of that!" Now she remembered clearly the events of the past evening. The flowerpots were no more. "Oh, golly!" she said again. "Whatever will I tell the witch!"

This problem, however, was temporarily forgotten at the sight of Mr. Beanpot advancing toward her, blowing out his cheeks with an important air.

"Just the person I wanta see!" he shouted, before he was near enough to talk in normal tones. When he got up close, he said, in a much quieter voice—in fact, in almost a whisper, "Your mother home, sis?"

Minx stared at him with a bold eye, although inside

she was quaking like a pot of boiling witch's brew. "My mother is asleep, and I wouldn't advise you or anyone else to wake her up, either!"

Mr. Beanpot mopped his red face, nervously. "I guess I'd better come back when she's awake," he mumbled. "When will that be?"

"She sleeps all day long," said Minx, pertly, "and then she goes out in the evening."

Mr. Beanpot's pale little eyes lighted up with a knowing look. "On her broomstick, I suppose!" he said.

The Birthday Cake

Now it was Minx's turn to flush and look upset. "None of your p's and q's!" she snapped.

"Never mind the sass, sis," said Mr. Beanpot, menacingly. "As you pro'ly know, all the missing children turned up last night to gladden their parents' grieving bosoms, though for the life of me I can't see why Mr. and Mrs. Martin—" he gave himself a shake. "But be that as it may—they all turned up last night VE-RY MYS-TER-I-OUS-LY! And—" he shoved his nose in Minx's face. "I think you know somepin about it!"

Minx drew back, haughtily. "Prove it!"

"All I know is what I heard from Billy Martin—" as he pronounced this name, a violent shudder passed over him; but he went on, courageously. "It's VE-RY STRANGE that those missin' kids found themselves in your house las' night with no remembrance of what went before!"

"Wouldn't you like to talk to my mother about it?" Minx invited, slyly.

Mr. Beanpot began to mop his face again, feverishly. "N-no, thank you! I'll come back some other time!" He turned and marched off as fast as his dignity would permit.

Little Witch

In spite of her anxiety, Minx snickered. "Old scaredy-cat!" she muttered.

"Oh dear!" she sighed. "Trouble, trouble, and more trouble! Oh dear! If there was only someone I could talk to about this!"

Suddenly she thought of Frances's great-grandma, and a gay lightness seized her. "Maybe she can help!"

She felt her clothes to see if they were dry. The wind was brisk and the sun bright, but her clothes were not quite dry. She felt terribly impatient, however, and snatching them from the tree, slipped into them swiftly.

When she was at last on her way to Frances's house, she shivered in the damp clothing, but she ran swiftly; so that when she finally arrived, she was warm and quite out of breath.

Frances opened the door. "Oh, Minx!" she cried, joyfully. "I'm so glad you could come over! Did you bring your broom?"

Minx opened her mouth in dismay. "Oh, Frances, I forgot! Besides, I'd better hide my broom for a while."

"Why? What's the matter?" asked Frances.

"Plenty!" said Minx, darkly. "I thought maybe your grandma could tell me what to do."

The Birthday Cake

"Tell you what to do!" repeated Frances, wonderingly. "You sure sound mysterious!"

"Well, I'll explain; but do you think your grandma would mind me telling her my troubles?"

"Goodness no!" said Frances. "Grandma listens to everybody's troubles by the yard! C'mon in!"

Minx followed her friend inside, skirting around a red wagon, a jack-in-the-box, and a deflated football.

Grandma was in the midst of making a cake. "It's George's birthday," she explained, "and of course we have to have a cake!"

"Chocolate," said George, sticking a fat finger in the batter.

"Take your finger out of that batter!" said Grandma, sharply. "Go wash your hands!"

"They're clean, Grandma," said George. "I licked them off."

"Goodness," said Grandma, to Minx. "I actually got out my paints today to start a water color, and then I remembered about the cake! Well!" she heaved a sigh. "Tomorrow's another day!"

"Grandma," said Frances, "Minx would like to tell you her troubles."

"If you're not too busy," added Minx, shyly.

Grandma looked at her kindly. "Of course I'm not too busy, darling! If you don't mind my working while you talk, fire away!"

Her words almost tumbling over one another, Minx told Grandma about the flowerpots and Mr. Beanpot, the detective.

"I'm afraid he'll put me in jail," she said. "It wasn't my fault that the children were turned into flowerpots; but I guess he'd never believe that. And what shall I do when my mother finds out the flowerpots are gone?"

Grandma was whisking the batter out into the greased tins. Minx thought she had not listened to a word. But then she said, "I think you haven't a thing to worry about in the case of Mr. Beanpot. He can't prove anything, and as long as those children can't recall what happened to them, you're safe. Anyway, you're just a child and they couldn't put you in jail. As for your mother, when she finds out the flowerpots are gone, that's something else again!"

As she was shoving the tins in the oven, a worried frown creased her forehead. "Maybe you'd better stay with us, my child. Just for a while, anyway. Wouldn't your mother let you come for a visit?"

The Birthday Cake

Minx shook her head, sadly. "Goodness! If she ever even found out I had friends, she'd be simply furious!"

"Well then, the only thing I can advise is for you to come here in case she wants to punish you too severely."

"Maybe you could hide here for a while," suggested Frances.

"I guess that would be against the law," said Grandma, regretfully. "No, I suppose I'm not much help, but I can only tell Minx to hope that her mother won't discover that the flowerpots are gone."

"Couldn't you get some other flowerpots that look just like them?" said Frances.

"My mother could tell the difference in a flash," said Minx. "Anyway, thanks for letting me tell you about it. At least I won't worry anymore about going to jail."

"If they put the witch in jail, then you won't have to worry about the flowerpots any more!" said Frances, brightly.

"Oh, that's right!" cried Minx, her face shining with new hope.

"Well anyway," said Grandma, "it's a good thing you came over, Minx, because now you can stay and have some of George's birthday cake."

"Ice cream, too!" said George, happily.

Little Witch

Minx forgot all her worries for the rest of the day. She had never eaten ice cream before, and thought she could never get enough of it. The chocolate cake was so light and rich, it almost melted away as soon as it was put in the mouth.

After the party, all the children ran out to play. By this time Minx's clothes were dry, and Frances had loaned her a warm jacket to wear.

She and Frances were having a joyful time playing hopscotch when Mrs. Sputter, president of the Parent-Teacher Association, came along. Mrs. Sputter was a very large lady, wearing square spectacles with a gold chain dangling from them, and she often made the statement that she was afraid of neither man, woman, nor beast.

When she saw the girls, she stopped and called out, in commanding tones, "You're Minikin Snickasnee, are you not? Come here, my child!"

Minx was standing on one foot in a square, about to leap to the next square; but so forceful was Mrs. Sputter, that she quickly obeyed.

"My dear," said Mrs. Sputter, fixing Minx with a look that was meant to be kindly, but which rooted her to the spot in terror, "I am the president of the P.T.A. and I notice that your mother does not belong!"

Minx gulped. "N-no ma'am!"

"Well, my dear, I think it is the duty of every mother to belong to the P.T.A., and I am going right straight to your house this minute to ask your mother to join!"

As Minx watched the large figure marching away toward Madam Snickasnee's house, she felt that now indeed her troubles were tumbling on her head in good measure.

8

MRS. SPUTTER

Minx knew she ought to run after Mrs. Sputter to try to stop her; but she was such a determined-looking lady, that Minx knew that nothing she had to say would be of any use.

When finally she was able to wiggle her tongue again, she said, "Just wait'll my mother meets up with her! Mrs. Sputter is gonna be awful sorry!"

"Mrs. Sputter doesn't believe in witches," said Frances.

Minx hooted. "She doesn't! Oh, golly! Just wait!"

Then she turned two shades paler. "But just wait till my mother meets up with me, too," she said, in a small voice.

"Do you really think she'll mind that you go to school?" asked Frances.

"I *know* it," said Minx, with conviction.

Billy Martin chose this moment to come along. "Yah! Ol' witch!" he taunted. "I'm rackin' my brains to put two and two together—jest you wait!"

"If you have to rack your brains to put two and two together, you better go back to the first grade!" retorted Minx, saucily.

Billy could think of no suitable reply to this; so he stuck out his tongue and sauntered off with a self-important air.

Mr. Beanpot, who happened to be coming along at

that moment, saw him and ducked hastily down a side street.

The town clock struck five, and Minx gave a little jump. "Oh, goodness! I've gotta get home! Oh, my goodness!"

"Do you want me to—to go with you?" offered Frances, bravely.

"Oh, no!" said Minx. "I wouldn't want anything to happen to *you!* Well, so long, Frances, thanks for everything. Here's your jacket."

"Keep it," said Frances. "I have two others. I know Grandma would like you to have it."

"Well, thanks! So long now!" And away Minx flew through the swiftly rising darkness.

When she went fearfully inside the house, the very first sight that greeted her eyes was a large flowerpot standing in the center of the table. The plant which grew from it was broad-leaved and luxuriant—a good deal like a thriving rubber plant.

Minx stared at it in horror. "Oh, my golly!" she said. "Mrs. Sputter!"

Then she became aware of Madam Snickasnee who was glaring at her evilly from a corner of the room.

"Right!" she croaked. "Your P.T.A. friend, Mrs. Sputter. Of all the pushy, obnoxious females, she was the worst! But I must say she makes a nice bit of green in the room."

She fixed Minx with her little red eyes, and said, ominously, "Who gave you permission to set foot inside that schoolhouse, miss?"

"I—I wanted to see what it was like," stammered Minx.

Little Witch

"Oh! You did!" sneered Madam Snickasnee. "And I suppose you've been lallygagging around with your fine school friends? Future flowerpots they'll be, or I'll eat my hat!"

Minx reflected that Madam Snickasnee's hat would make quite a few, and anything but tasty mouthfuls; but she was soon rudely jarred from this train of thought.

"And another thing," said Madam Snickasnee, advancing toward Minx, slowly, her eyes gleaming like hot coals, "another thing, miss! Where are those flowerpots?"

Minx longed desperately to rush for the door, but her

knees felt much too weak. But what with thinking about this problem so much, she had her story all ready.

"A detective was around asking about the missing children," she said, hoping her voice wouldn't quaver; "so I got scared he'd suspect about the flowerpots, and I hid them."

Madam Snickasnee seemed a bit taken aback. "A detective snooping around here?"

"Yes," said Minx. "His name is Mr. Beanpot."

"Well! Well!" Her eyes narrowed into slits. "That certainly is very interesting! In fact I'll be very interested to know the next time he comes around here!"

"Y-yes, Ma'am! I'll be sure to tell you!"

"And now, miss," continued Madam Snickasnee, "pray tell me where you hid the flowerpots."

Minx felt a cold sweat break out on her forehead. Why hadn't she thought about that? But she had to say something. The witch's eyes were almost burning a hole right through her. Boldly, she said, "I put them out in the yard!"

"Well, all I have to say," croaked Madam Snickasnee, "is that they'd better be there when I look for them tomorrow!"

"Oh, they'll be there," said Minx, "un—unless some-one s-stole them!"

"Oh, stole them, hey?" shrieked the witch. "Don't start making excuses, miss. They'd just better be there!"

She slung a leg over her broom, and whizzed off into the darkness.

"Oh, golly! Now I *am* in for something!" groaned Minx. "She'll be sure to look for those flowerpots when she comes home."

She suddenly thought of the beautiful lady whom she had not glimpsed for two days; so she went over to the mirror. For a long time she gazed into its blurred depths, and then suddenly she saw her—beautiful as a star, smiling at her with tenderness.

She was afraid to turn around to try to find her, for then the lovely image would fade from the mirror.

For the first time, she spoke to the reflection, for now she was sure that this was a real person, and not just an imaginary one.

"Oh, beautiful lady," she said, "can't you help me? The witch will surely do something terrible to me when she finds out the flowerpots are gone!"

Instantly, there was a sound as of the mirror cracking,

and the image wavered and melted away. Minx's heart sank like a stone. Slowly, with tears in her dark eyes, she turned away, and then gave a start of surprise.

There before her was the lady of the mirror! But a thousand times more beautiful than her reflection! Her hair streamed down to the floor, silver-pale as quiet water at dusk, crowned with a circlet of stars; her eyes were dark and luminous like shadowed forest pools; her skin as white and pink as the petals of arbutus. Tall and slender she was, wrapped around in a mantle of glowing silver.

For a long moment Minx could do nothing but stare. Then, in a voice that was almost a whisper, she said, "Who are you?"

But the lady never spoke. She just shook her head, slowly, and pressed a finger against her lovely mouth. At first Minx was bewildered. Then she said, "Oh! Can't you speak?"

Again the beautiful creature shook her head.

Minx felt very sad. "How can we understand each other then? Won't you be able to help me?"

The lady looked sorrowful, too; but this time, she nodded her head, as if to say "yes."

Little Witch

Suddenly, there was a rap on the door, and the lady looked around in alarm.

"Don't be scared," said Minx, comfortingly. "That's probably my friends. We're trying to get the right magic brew to make a fairy appear."

The lady looked as if she were laughing. Her eyes were full of mirth, and her face dimpled.

Minx hurried to open the door. There stood Frances, with her brothers and sister.

"Come in!" she cried, eagerly. "Come in and meet the beautiful lady!"

"Beautiful lady?" repeated the children, questioningly. They all piled in, looking around curiously.

"Where is any beautiful lady?" demanded Jack.

"I don't see anyone," said Bob.

"Why she's right th—" began Minx; then gave a gasp. "Oh, goodness! She's gone!"

"You're just kidding us, aren't you?" said Jack.

"No—honest I'm not! She was the most beautiful lady in the whole world! But she couldn't talk."

"Deaf and dumb," said Bob.

"No," said Minx, "she could hear me; but she couldn't speak."

"Well, anyway, she's just disappeared," said Frances, "so she must be magic."

"Maybe she's an enchanted lady like in the fairy stories," said Alice.

Minx looked at Alice with wonder. "Why Alice, you certainly are a smart little girl! That's probably just what she is!"

"Then let's get to work on the magic brew," said Jack, "and maybe we'll discover something to get rid of her enchantment."

"That's called disenchanting someone," said Frances.

"O.K.," said Jack, agreeably, "but whatever it's called, let's get started."

9

THE YELLOW POWDER

"Well, what bottle will it be this time?" said Minx, looking over the colorful bottles.

All the children began to clamor for a chance to choose.

"I have an idea," said Frances, sensibly. "Why don't you just shut your eyes, Minx, and I'll turn you around three times, and then you pick one."

"O.K! That sounds like a good idea," said Minx. She squeezed her eyes shut, and Frances turned her around three times, so that she was facing the shelves.

"Golly, I feel dizzy!" giggled Minx, reaching out her

hand hesitantly toward the shelves. She curled her fingers around a jar. "Here it is, I guess!"

"O.K! Open your eyes!" said Frances.

"Oh my!" said Alice. "That's surely a pretty yellow!"

Minx took the yellow powder and dumped a little into the magic kettle, along with some magic liquid.

Immediately, the ingredients boiled up into a seething mass, like frothing sunshine.

"Oh, how beautiful!" cried Frances.

"Shhh!" said Bob. "Something's happening!"

"What is it?" whispered George, hoarsely.

The vapor was winding mysteriously around the room, and the children saw a form emerging. They felt as if they hardly dared to breathe.

The vapor began clearing away, and there, perched on the edge of the kettle, was a tiny creature about eight inches high, with wide gold butterfly wings, and a pointed, saucy face! She was dressed in a filmy gown of palest gold, and around her long, golden hair was a wreath of tiny blue flowers that just matched her eyes.

The children all stood around, mouths open, eyes popping. At last Minx said in a voice that was hardly more than a squeak, "You're—you're a fairy!"

Little Witch

In a voice as thin as a sliver of rain, the fairy said, "Of course! Could you mistake me for anything else?"

"Oh! How beautiful!" said Alice, in awe.

The fairy preened herself. "Of course I'm beautiful! I have no less than six elves courting me right now, and I would have seven, only that little hussy Bluebell tricked him into marrying her by pretending she owned twelve beehives!"

She stamped her little foot, indignantly.

"Well, anyway," said Frances, soothingly, "I think six elves is an awful lot."

The Yellow Powder

The fairy looked mollified. "What did you want to see me about?" she asked, amiably, settling herself on the edge of the kettle, and swinging her feet.

"As a matter of fact, nothing," said Minx. "We just wanted to see a fairy."

The fairy reached into a small bag which swung from her belt, and took out a tiny lipstick and mirror. "You couldn't have chosen a better fairy to look at than me," she said, smugly, beginning to paint her lips with great care.

The children were so fascinated that they crowded quite close.

"Good heavens!" cried the fairy. "You get so close I can hardly breathe!"

The children moved back just a little, never taking their eyes from her.

"Don't you want any magic at all?" demanded the fairy, rather disappointed.

"Maybe she could think of a way of dis—disenchant the beautiful lady," suggested Alice.

"Bring on the enchantments!" said the fairy boastfully. "I'll fix 'em all! Who is the unfortunate creature who needs to be disenchanted?"

Little Witch

Minx told her all about the lady of the mirror.

The fairy's eyes grew quite round. "Oh, my goodness!" she piped. "I know that lady well, my dear! And I know all about the enchantments, too. She's under a spell placed on her by Madam Snickasnee—"

"My mother!" cried Minx, in astonishment.

"Don't interrupt," said the fairy, crossly. "This enchantment can never be broken until—" All at once her voice faded out so weakly that no one could hear her any more, and then she faded out, too.

"Oh, my golly!" cried Minx, in disappointment. "Let's hurry and throw some more powder in the kettle!"

They rushed to the jar, but as they reached for it, they heard a dreadful racket and clatter outside the door.

"What's that?" they cried, fearfully.

Scarcely were the words spoken, when in through the door burst Madam Snickasnee!

"AHAAA!" screeched the witch, in a long, drawn-out howl, while the children stood rooted to the floor, their knees knocking.

Minx was the first to recover sufficiently to speak. "Oh, hello, Ma'am," she quavered, "these are my f-friends from school."

The Yellow Powder

Madam Snickasnee looked at them as if she thought less than nothing of them.

"Oh! Your fine school friends!" she sneered.

"How do you do," said Frances, weakly.

The other children opened their mouths, but no sounds emerged.

"Don't ask me how I do!" shrieked Madam Snickasnee so violently that they all backed away in terror. "I do fine! But I'd do much better without all these gawking brats around!"

She grabbed Minx by the ear and held fast. "You, young lady! What were you doing with my magic kettle out? Speak up!"

"I—I was trying s-some experiments, Ma'am!"

"Oh, experiments, hey? And may I ask what experiment resulted from all your brazen fiddle-faddling with my magic powders?"

"N-nothing much, Ma'am," squeaked Minx.

Madam Snickasnee pushed Minx roughly aside, and went over to the kettle. Sticking her long nose inside, she took a deep sniff.

"AHA!" she screamed. "I smell the yellow powder! What did that little snip of a fairy tell you?"

"Nothing, Ma'am. She just showed off, and put lip-stick-on."

The witch narrowed her eyes until they were red slits. "I suspect you lie, little vixen!"

George began to howl. "I wanna go home!"

"George wants to go home," Frances spoke up bravely. "Good night, everybody!"

"Just a minute!" screamed Madam Snickasnee. "Nobody's going to set foot outside that door!"

Alice began to howl, too. There was such a din what with Madam Snickasnee screeching, and George and Alice howling, that Minx stuck her fingers in her ears.

"You brat!" shrieked Madam Snickasnee. "How dare you plug up your ears when I'm speaking!"

Minx took her fingers out of her ears.

"And another thing!" the witch went on, in the same tone of voice. "I happened to see Billy Martin while on my travels this evening—so I'm quite sure now what happened to those flowerpots! You were sneaking around in my magic powders, and found the formula!"

She grabbed Minx by the ear again. "Now just for that, Miss Smarty, you're going to do a little job for me! We still have that bottle of Black Spell Brew you made

The Yellow Powder

up the other night—so now you'll take it and change all your wonderful friends into beautiful flowerpots!"

All the children let out gasps and screeches.

"Oh, Ma'am!" cried Minx. "Please, please don't make me do that! Oh, please, please, Ma'am!"

But Madam Snickasnee got the bottle of Black Spell Brew, and uncorking it, thrust it into Minx's hand. "Get busy, or I'll change you first into a flowerpot, and all your fine friends after you!"

"I wanna go home!" bellowed George and Alice.

"I guess you'd better do it, Minx," said Frances, as bravely as she could. "We'll get changed into flowerpots, anyhow."

"Please don't make me do it, Ma'am," begged Minx, beginning to cry. "They're good children. Let them go home!"

"I don't care whether they're good or bad," said Madam Snickasnee. "They're children, and that's enough! Start now, young lady, or you'll be sorry!"

Slowly, with shaking hand, Minx tipped up the bottle over the blond head of Frances. But just as the liquid started to ooze out thickly, there sounded a knock on the door.

Madam Snickasnee gave a start of surprise.

"Who can that be?" she croaked.

"Open it," said Minx, eagerly, holding the bottle upright again, before any of the liquid could spill.

"There's no one I want to see," said the witch. "They can just go away!"

"Maybe it's your new poison catalog," suggested Minx, anxiously.

"That would come in the mail, stupid," said the witch.

Minx's heart started to sink again. If only something would happen to save them!

But at that moment, the door burst open and in walked Mr. Beanpot with two policemen!

"The witch is going to change us to flowerpots!" sobbed George.

"Not I! Never! Never!" screeched Madam Snicksnee, and pointing a clawlike finger at Minx, she said, "That horrible child was going to do it!"

"Well," said Mr. Beanpot, suspiciously, "something funny is going on here, and we arrest both of you in the name of the law!"

"Quick, Minx, quick!" shrieked Madam Snickasnee. "Pour the Black Spell Brew on them!"

Little Witch

But quite deliberately, Minx dropped the bottle on the floor, and all the brew spilled out.

Scorcher bolted over to it in a flash and started to lap it up. But no sooner had he taken two laps, than he gave a hideous yowl, and turned into a puff of black smoke which quickly disappeared.

"Oh my cat! My beautiful cat!" howled Madam Snickasnee. "That's the end of him, poor dear creature!"

"Never mind that," said the bigger policeman. "Come along quietly, now."

So Madam Snickasnee and Minx were taken off to jail.

10

GRANDMA TO THE RESCUE

With a clang, the door of the jail shut them in, and they heard the scrunch of the big key in the lock.

Madam Snickasnee had screamed and threatened all the way, and now for a while she tore around, cursing and shrieking; but then, seeing that it did her no good, she sank down on one of the bunks and began to mutter darkly.

Minx was sitting miserably on the other bunk, unhappy, less because she was in jail than because she was shut in the same cell with the witch.

"A pretty pickle," Madam Snickasnee kept mumbling. "Me, the smartest, cleverest witch this side of the Rockies, to allow mere men to get the best of me—and one of them a man by the name of 'Beanpot,' too. Ugh!"

And she shuddered with such violence that the bunk rattled.

"Why don't you try some magic?" suggested Minx, timidly.

"Without my magic pot or powders, or even my catalog?" said Madam Snickasnee, fiercely. "You stupid child! This is all your fault, too, and I'll not forget it, either, once I get out of this loathsome place!"

All of a sudden they heard voices.

"Ha!" said Madam Snickasnee, triumphantly. "Here they come to let me out, and when that happens, you'd better shiver and shake, for your fate will be worse than jail!"

Minx was shivering and shaking already.

Presently a big policeman stopped by their cell. When Minx saw who was with him, the icicle in her chest melted away—for it was Frances's grandma!

"Well, little girl," said the policeman, "this lady has come to take you home with her."

"You're not leaving me here alone, are you?" screamed Madam Snickasnee.

"That we are, Ma'am," said the policeman, "and I'm sure you'll be nice and cozy till tomorrow when the judge will take up your case."

Madam Snickasnee began to scream and threaten again while Grandma led Minx out of the jail house.

"You have to appear in court tomorrow, too, darling," said Grandma, "but I persuaded the judge to let you come home with me tonight."

Little Witch

Minx clung tightly to Grandma's hand all the way home. She had never had a hand to cling to before in her whole life.

The children were noisy with delight to see her, and even though it was rather late, they all got out of bed, and Grandma fed them milk and sandwiches. Minx ate and ate, and then all of a sudden everything began to blur—the cheerful, lighted room, the rosy, laughing faces, and her head dropped down on her chest. She was fast asleep.

The first thing she saw in the morning was Frances's tousled blond head on the pillow next to her. Frances was still asleep, her eyelashes light on her flushed cheeks, her mouth partly open.

Minx gazed at her intently, a warm feeling inside her. How wonderful it was to have a friend like Frances, and to be able to share a family like this one, even a little bit!

Suddenly Frances's gray eyes opened, and she smiled sleepily at Minx.

"Grandma put you to bed last night. It's fun having you here with us."

"I wish—I wish I could stay here forever," said Minx, fervently.

Grandma to the Rescue

A knock sounded on the door, and Frances called, "Come in!"

Grandma came bustling into the room. "Get up, girls. Minx has to get down to the courthouse early. I have her bath all ready for her."

"Bath?" repeated Minx, in alarm.

"Didn't you ever take a bath?" asked Frances, in astonishment.

"No, I never did."

"Well, now you're going to," said Grandma, firmly, "and I bet you'll enjoy it. So march straight into the bathroom!"

Minx marched, and after stripping off the nightgown Frances had loaned her, she got into the tub with great timidity.

The water closed around in delicious warmth.

Grandma called through the door, "Take the washcloth and soap and give yourself a good scrubbing! Don't leave one speck of dirt!"

Minx scrubbed, lightly at first, and then with greater gusto. The water promptly became as black as Madam Snickasnee's hat, and at last Minx stepped forth as clean and shiny as a new dime.

"Are you finished yet?" Frances asked. "I'm coming in with your clothes."

Minx hated to think of putting on her ragged, dirty clothes against her clean skin, so when Frances handed her a pile of clean, whole clothing, she was overjoyed.

"These are mine, and may be a bit big for you," said Frances, "but I'm sure they'll do for now."

Minx scrambled gaily into the clothes, and finally pulled on a starched yellow dress.

"Oh, my!" she said. "This is the most beautiful dress I ever saw!"

Frances laughed heartily. "This is just an old dress of mine!"

"It doesn't look old to me," Minx said, her face shining with happiness, as well as cleanliness.

"Now come on to my room, and I'll fix your hair," said Frances.

At last Minx was all dressed, from neat, shining hair, to toes—although the shoes were rather large. After breakfast her stomach was comfortably full of pancakes, sausages, and milk.

"We can't waste another minute," said Grandma, clapping on a gay hat with a large red bow and quan-

tities of cherries. "I've got to take you straight to the courthouse!"

"I feel scared," said Minx.

"Oh, nonsense!" said Grandma. "There's nothing for you to feel scared about. Come along!"

The whole family went, all piling into the car which was supposed to hold only five people. But Alice sat on

Frances's lap, and George scrooged down on the floor.

It looked as if the whole town had heard about the trial, because streams of people were pouring into the courthouse.

Minx had to go sit up front; but Grandma and the children could find seats only in the back.

Pretty soon Judge Honk came in, and everyone stood up. Then he sat down, and so did everyone else.

There were other cases to be tried, and the children found it all quite dull; but at last Madam Snickasnee was called up.

"What is the charge?" asked the judge.

"Witchcraft, your Honor," said the prosecuting attorney.

"Be specific, please," said the judge. "That is a very serious charge."

"The accused has been observed riding around on a broomstick, your Honor, and there is also the matter of the seven missing children who were finally discovered coming out of the accused's house. Then there is also the mysterious disappearance of Mrs. Algernon Sputter for whom all the little Sputters mourn night and day." Here the prosecuting attorney paused to wipe away the tears which were streaming from his pale, prominent eyes.

"Go on," said Judge Honk. "What makes you think the accused had anything to do with the disappearance of Mrs. Sputter?"

"She was last seen going into the accused's house," said the prosecuting attorney, importantly.

The judge turned to Madam Snickasnee.

"Are these accusations true?" he asked.

Madam Snickasnee drew herself up haughtily. "I'm as innocent as a spotless lamb," she said, indignantly. Then she made such an effort to smile sweetly, that her cheeks creaked, and almost split.

"If I lie about this," she went on, pretending to wipe a tear away from her eye, "may I turn into a—an ant-eater!"

Instantly, before the astonished eyes of all the spectators, there stood an anteater, plumy-tailed, squat, its long tongue flicking around for ants.

As soon as Judge Honk was able to speak again, he said, "Well, I— I guess that finishes this case. If the defendant happens to resume her natural form, the court will have to sentence her to prison. Meanwhile, you'd

better take this—this creature to the zoo. Next case!"

As two astounded policemen led the anteater from the courtroom, Minx was called up.

"What is the charge against the defendant?" asked Judge Honk.

"Witchcraft, your Honor," said the prosecuting attorney, looking at Minx rather nervously, as if he expected another anteater to appear any moment.

"Be specific, please," said the judge.

"The defendant was seen riding on a broomstick, and

one Billy Martin (Judge Honk winced) has stated that she was present in the house when he and the other formerly missing children found themselves again."

Judge Honk looked at Minx sternly.

"What have you to say for yourself, young lady?" he asked.

Minx could feel her knees shaking, but she said, bravely, "It's true I can ride on a broomstick. I learned it from my mother. But I had nothing to do with the disappearance of Billy Martin or the others. In fact, I had them brought back again."

"How did they disappear in the first place?" asked Judge Honk.

Minx answered promptly, "My mother changed them into flowerpots—and Mrs. Sputter, too!"

Everyone in the courtroom gasped.

"But I found a formula," Minx continued, "that made the Pied Piper appear, and he piped a tune that made all the flowerpots change back again."

"Could you do that for Mrs. Sputter, too?" asked the judge.

"I—I could try," said Minx, doubtfully.

"As you're a child," said Judge Honk, "this court will

not hold you responsible for any witchcraft you may have committed. Just turn over a new leaf, and be law-abiding in the future."

"Yes, sir!" said Minx, thankfully.

Judge Honk pounded with his gavel. "Case dismissed! Court adjourned until two o'clock this afternoon!"

11

THE MAGIC MIRROR

Grandma and the children were waiting for Minx, and she was soundly hugged and kissed by all of them. As they were going out of the courthouse, Minx gave a little cry.

"What's the matter?" asked Frances.

"I thought I saw the beautiful lady!" said Minx. "She went out the door just ahead of us!"

"Oh, you got a good imagination!" scoffed Jack.

"Maybe," said Minx, "but I was almost sure!"

"Well now you must come home with us," said Grandma, "and be part of our family."

"Oh golly!" cried Minx. "Do you really mean it?"

"Of course she does," said Frances. "But Grandma, let's first go to Minx's house and get the magic powders and stuff."

"Yeah, it's a shame to waste all that good stuff," said Bob.

"Maybe we can see more fairies," said Alice.

"Well, you know that Judge Honk doesn't want you to practice any more witchcraft, Minx," said Grandma, worriedly.

"Oh, Grandma," begged Frances, "he won't mind if we take those few little things!"

So Grandma drove to Minx's house, and they all went in and carried out the jars of magic powders, the kettle, and the brooms.

When they were making their last trip, Minx said, "Say! Mrs. Sputter is gone!"

Sure enough! The large plant was missing from the table.

"The spell must have broken when my mother was changed into the anteater," said Minx.

"Well, let's not worry about Mrs. Sputter," said Frances. "It's almost lunch time and I'm starved."

"Would you mind waiting for me just one minute?"

asked Minx. "Let me alone here, and I won't be long, I promise!"

"What do you want to do?" asked Frances, curiously.

"I can't tell you," said Minx. "Please don't be mad at me, Frances, but I just can't."

"Oh I don't mind," said Frances, good-naturedly, and she went out quickly, glancing back only once to say, "But hurry, because I'm starved!"

Minx went over to the old bureau and gazed into the dirty, cracked mirror.

"Oh, beautiful lady," she whispered, "please let me see you again!"

Immediately, the shining, tender face appeared. Minx turned around swiftly, and was enraptured to see the lovely creature standing there, smiling at her with deep kindliness.

Minx felt a great glowing warmth fill her whole body, and words she had never spoken before in her life spilled out. "Oh, I love you!" she said.

Then the lady held out her slender arms, and gathered Minx into them.

"At last the spell is broken," she said, in a voice that was like clear streams and meadows bright with sunshine.

Little Witch

"It's rather a long story, and I don't care to keep your good friends waiting."

"Oh, don't go away, please don't go away," begged Minx.

"I promise you will see me again very soon," said the lady. "Believe me, my child. Now join your friends."

It didn't take Grandma long to get home; fortunately, because they all had so much of Madam Snickasnee's equipment piled on top of them.

For lunch they had scrambled eggs, hamburgers, and gingerbread with whipped cream on top.

Then afterwards Grandma took Minx to town to buy her some clothes.

"I feel like a brand new girl," said Minx, as they got back in the car with all their packages.

Suddenly she gave a squeal. "Oh, Grandma! There's Mrs. Sputter!"

There indeed was Mrs. Sputter, marching down the street, surrounded by three little Sputters, all happily chattering and beaming. Mrs. Sputter, however, had a rather dazed look about her. When she saw Minx she gave a little scream, and clapped a hand to her plump bosom.

"Stay away from me! Don't come near me, you witch child!" she shrieked.

Minx got into the car hastily, having no desire, anyway, to go near Mrs. Sputter.

Grandma, however, went up to her, holding out her hand.

"It's so nice to see you again, Mrs. Sputter. It's too bad you were under that nasty spell. But I assure you that Minx had nothing to do with it."

"Well, I suppose she didn't," said Mrs. Sputter, doubtfully. "I hear I was a flowerpot," she added, with a shudder. "All I know is, all of a sudden I was sitting on that frightful woman's filthy table in the midst of a lot of dirty dishes and a pot of stewed frogs. Ugh! I didn't have any idea how I got there, but I can tell you I got home to my dear ones as fast as I could go! What an experience!" She fanned herself violently with a large lavender handkerchief.

"Yes, it was certainly terrible," agreed Grandma, "but now everything is all right again, isn't it?"

"Unless that horrible woman regains her former shape!" said Mrs. Sputter, in apprehension.

"Well, let's worry about that when the time comes," said Grandma. "But meantime Minx is going to live with us, and if you and the other people of this town could help her forget her former unpleasant associations, perhaps she could be happy for the first time in her life."

"Yes, well, I guess you're right," said Mrs. Sputter, glancing at Minx, nervously. "I must be getting home now. Good-bye!"

That evening, Grandma confided to Frances that she was worried.

"I'm afraid the people here won't forget that Minx was a witch's child," she said.

"Billy Martin was teasing her again today," said Frances. "He was hollering 'Witch's child, ol' witch's child! Your mother's an ol' witch anteater!'"

The Magic Mirror

"That boy!" said Grandma, shaking her head. "He should be kept too busy to get into mischief!"

"He ought to be put in jail," said Frances, darkly.

After all the supper dishes were cleared away, Grandma got out her paints to do some more work on a landscape she had started about six months before.

"I just never seem to be able to finish this," she said, "what with one thing and another."

"And now you have six children, Grandma," said George.

"That's just fine," said Grandma, smiling at Minx. "It's always nice to have an even number, don't you think so? Three boys and three girls, and now Frances has a sister near her own age."

But before she even had any of her paints mixed, the bell rang.

"Now who can that be?" wondered Grandma; but all the children had already gone to find out.

As soon as the door was flung open, Minx gave a cry of joy.

"Oh! The beautiful lady!"

All the other children just stood there, mouths open in astonishment. They had never before seen anyone so lovely.

"Well, may I come in?" asked the lady, smiling.

"Oh, yes! yes!" cried Minx, catching her hand and drawing her inside.

"Oh, my!" said Grandma, when she saw the lady. "I know it's not polite to make personal remarks, but I never saw anyone so beautiful as you, not even in my imagination!"

"Thank you," said the lady. "And now let me tell you my name. It is *Moonfire,* and if you will all gather around me I'll tell you a story."

"Oh, a story! Goodie!" cried George and Alice.

"What kinda story is it?" demanded Jack. "Any cowboys in it?"

"Be quiet, children," said Grandma. "Everyone sit down and be comfortable, and while Moonfire is telling the story I'll get on with my painting."

"Don't you want to listen too, Grandma?" asked George.

"I can listen while I paint," said Grandma. "Naturally I'd never want to miss a story."

So the beautiful lady sat on the couch with Minx and the children crowding around her.

"In the first place," she began, in her clear, sparkling

voice, "perhaps you people should know that I am a fairy."

They all shrieked. "But I thought fairies were teeny weeny things!" cried Alice.

"Yes, many of them are, but there are different tribes of fairies," explained Moonfire. "I am a nymph, and nymphs are the same size as humans. Besides, they are really much better."

"Why?" asked Minx.

"Well, I'm sure I don't know," said Moonfire, "except that we nymphs are all brought up to believe so. Anyway, you mustn't interrupt. My story begins about eight years ago. I was walking through the woods with my child, who was just a baby then, when I happened to meet the witch Madam Snickasnee who was digging around for poisonous roots and herbs to use in her spells. As soon as I saw her I decided that the best thing for me to do was to hurry away as quickly as possible; but unfortunately she saw me. 'Oh! A beauteous nymph!' she croaked, sarcastically. 'Why are you in such a hurry, fair creature? Don't you like my company?'

"I should have kept right on going, but foolishly I turned around and retorted, 'No, I don't care for your company, and you'd better keep out of our woods, or the fairies will get after you!'

" 'Oh! A snippy nymph!' she sneered. 'Well, you'll find you can't get high-handed with Madam Snickasnee!'

"Then I hurried away; but it was that very night she stirred up one of her wicked brews; because I was awakened from my sleep by a vision of her bending over her pot, stirring, and cackling,

> 'Boil and bubble,
> Boil and brew!
> Now I cast a spell
> On you!'

"Then she said, 'From now on I will take care of your child for you, and bring her up with a witch's tender care. And you will never be able to speak to her until she says the words "I love you," and after my training I doubt if she'll even know such words!' And then she gave that hideous laugh.

"Oh, how unhappy I was when I found my darling little girl missing, and knew that none of the fairies' spells could break the old witch's enchantment!"

Minx was staring at her with wide, shining eyes. "You

don't mean— Oh, it couldn't be true! Is it really true?"

Moonfire smiled at her lovingly. "Yes, Minikin, it's really true. You are not a witch's child at all. You are the daughter of a nymph; my own child!"

"Oh, my own mother!" cried Minx, and once more she was in the lady's arms.

12

MOONFIRE

"But tell me one thing more," said Minx, "didn't I see you in the courthouse this morning?"

"You did," said Moonfire, "and it was I who changed Madam Snickasnee into an anteater."

All the children cried out in astonishment.

"Of course you know that fairies are well acquainted with magic," said Moonfire, "but what great good fortune when Madam Snickasnee told that lie in such a way that she played right into my hands! For perhaps you don't know that when a fairy catches a witch in a lie, the fairy has her in her power!"

"But how long will the spell last?" asked Minx, anxiously.

"It's a good strong spell," said Moonfire, "and will last the natural life of an anteater. At the end of that time she will be provided with a handsome funeral of which any anteater might be proud."

"So much has happened today," sighed Minx, "that my head is in a whirl. I'm sure I'll not get to sleep tonight."

"Well, I'm sure you'll try, at least," said Grandma, looking up from her painting. (She had a blue smudge on her nose which vividly brought out the blue of her eyes.) "And it's past your bedtime right now. Moonfire can stay and visit with me while you children get to bed."

"Thank you," said Moonfire, smiling graciously, "but I think I should like to go to bed myself. It's been rather a strenuous day. Casting spells can be so wearing!"

"You must come again soon," said Grandma, warmly. 'When would you like to take Minx back with you?"

"Oh, no need for that," said Moonfire, airily. "I'm going to stay here, now. I'm quite sure you could put me up all right, couldn't you?"

Grandma looked at her in frank amazement.

"Well, I—I do have an extra bedroom; but the house is a bit crowded right now, as it is—don't you think?"

Little Witch

"You would certainly find it to your advantage to take me in," said Moonfire. "I could go back to live in the forest comfortably enough, but I feel that since you were so kind to my child I owe it to you to stay here."

Grandma looked more amazed than ever. She thought, "What a funny way to repay anyone, to go live with them!"

But she said, "Oh, you needn't feel you owe me anything, Moonfire. Minx is a dear little girl, and it was a pleasure to take her in."

"Well, and I'm sure it will be a pleasure for you to take me in, too," Moonfire assured her. "But I am quite weary. Would you kindly show me my bedroom?"

The next day the news was all over town. Minx Snickasnee (now to be known only as "Minikin" which means "dainty and delicate") was not the child of a witch, after all, but the daughter of a nymph, the most beautiful creature ever seen.

The newspaper published a long account of the whole story, on page one, and now no longer could Minikin be considered a witch's child by anybody.

The mayor decided that the anteater, the former Madam Snickasnee, should not spend her days lolling at ease in the town zoo, but should earn her board and keep by cleaning out the ants in the ladies' kitchens whenever they became overrun with the pests.

"All my wishes have come true," said Minikin, as she and Frances walked home from school.

"Maybe because you're a fairy's child," said Frances.

When they entered the house, Frances said, "My goodness! Something's missing!"

"What?" asked Minikin.

"No scooter or skates lying around in the way! Everything neat as a pin!"

Grandma appeared in the living-room doorway, looking flushed and a bit dazed.

"Oh, girls, it's you! My goodness, I don't know whether I'm standing on my head or my feet! Do you notice how clean the house is?"

"Well, yes, we noticed," said Frances.

"It's all your mother's doings, Minikin."

"My mother?" cried Minikin, in surprise. "Does she like to clean house?"

"She doesn't do anything but play on a musical instrument she calls a lute, sing like an angel, and tat lace that looks like spun moonbeams. But when she claps her hands, the whole place becomes full of little elves and fairies who clean up the place as quick as a wink. Some of them are in the kitchen right this minute making supper!"

Before the girls even reached the kitchen, they were surrounded by the most heavenly odors of food cooking —smells of turkey, cake, pie, gingerbread—every good smell anyone could ever think of. There were three fairies in the kitchen, all engulfed in frilly aprons, mixing, peeling, boiling, and baking furiously. One of them paused long enough to smile at the girls, but went right back to work.

Moonfire came into the kitchen. Whenever she entered a room, the whole place seemed to become illumined with a light clearer than sunshine.

Minikin ran up to her and threw her arms around her. "Oh mother! How wonderful you are!"

Her mother smiled lovingly. "Just think how hard

you children worked with all those old powders to cause a fairy to appear, and I can bring in hundreds of them any time I want to!"

"From now on this whole house will be full of magic," said Frances, "good magic!"

"I found a much better use for the magic kettle than stirring up spells and strange creatures, too," said Moonfire. "I have said the magic words over it to turn it into a soup kettle. From now on soup will always be bubbling in it—the most nourishing kind of soup you could imagine, as well as the most delicious. The kettle can never become empty, and now all the poor, hungry people of this town and from anywhere in the world can come here and have as much soup as they want. I feel that this will be a good work for me instead of just singing and playing on the lute. I'll be pretty busy a good part of the time dishing up soup."

"Not too busy to pay a little attention to me, I hope?" said Minikin, jealously.

"Never too busy for that, my darling," said her mother, holding her close. "I have missed you so long that I have to make it up to you as well as to myself."

"Oh gosh I don't think another good thing could possibly happen!" sighed Frances.

"Yes it could," said Moonfire. "I'm sure you won't weep to hear that when Master Billy Martin came by today and started chalking up the front walk with rude comments concerning my daughter, I sent some elves out to settle him! They pinched him hard, and made him clear off all the words."

"Hurray!" cried the girls.

"I think perhaps he won't be bothering you any more," added Moonfire. "I even have a strong feeling that he and his mother will move out of this town!"

"And how wonderful everything is for Grandma now," said Frances. "She'll be able to paint like mad from morning till night!"

Just then Bob and Jack came running in. "Oh, golly! Who do you suppose is coming up the walk, girls?"

"Who?" asked Frances.

"Judge Honk, Mr. Bunch, and Mr. Beanpot!" said Jack. "Do you suppose they're gonna arrest Minikin again?"

"Maybe they've just come to call on my mother," said Minikin, nervously.

Both Jack and Bob lost no time in answering the bell. They did not want to miss any arrests, even when they occurred in their own family.

"Good day," said Mr. Beanpot, jovially, "would Miss Minikin be in?"

Timidly, Minikin came to the door.

"Miss Minikin," said Judge Honk, bowing low, "we should like to make a request of you."

"Yes, sir," said Minx, questioningly.

"Miss Minikin," said Judge Honk, "Mr. Beanpot, Mr. Bunch and I wondered—well, we'd consider it a great favor, Miss Minikin, if you'd be kind enough to let each of us take a ride or two on your broomstick!"

THE END